CHEESY
on the Inside

written and illustrated by
Kelly Rose Humphreys

Dedicated to my loving family, friends, teachers, and to all of those who have supported my passion for pizza.

There were four slices of pizza wearing toppings galore,
pepperonis, and garlic, and mushrooms, and more!

They were always together,
   these four ruled the school.
Everybody who knew them
   thought they were SO cool.

There was one slice of pizza
who didn't look the same.
He stood out from the others,
they saw him as "lame."

He was covered in ooey-gooey cheese
and nothing more.
That made him an easy target
for the other four.

The slices with toppings
  bullied the little slice of cheese.
They taunted him as he cried,
  "Just leave me alone please!"

They showed off their toppings
  they always got to wear.
They even threw some at him,
  mocking him for being bare.

One day, after the teasing…
    a black olive got stuck.
The little slice of cheese smiled
    at his sudden change in luck.

He collected the toppings that were thrown about…
    grinning bigger at each one.
He stuck them to his melty cheese,
    and squealed with joy, "Just wait until I'm done!"

The next day at school
  there was no little cheese slice.
He had the others fooled,
  they didn't think twice.

He played their pizza games,
  he laughed with his new friends...
but pretending to be someone you aren't is wrong
  And that is NOT how this story ends.

You see, later that day
  while the disguised little slice was with the other four,
he felt a few drops of rain sprinkle down—
  and then it really started to pour!

His olives slid off,
  the pineapple was gone…
His mushrooms were lost,
  the rain carried on…

The other slices began to panic,
  they were stunned by the mess.
They never saw what was coming…
  No one could have guessed!

All of the slices became totally soaked!
　　Their colorful toppings slid to the ground.
Now covered only in cheese,
　　they looked one another up and down.

They blinked in confusion…
　　they sat there in shock.
The slices couldn't move,
　　no one could talk.

They couldn't believe it,
　　they all looked the same!
Why didn't they see this sooner?
　　They hung their heads in shame.

The slices began apologizing
   for the mean things they used to say.
They all were grateful for the lesson
   that was taught that rainy day.

Remember the slices of pizza
   before you judge or try to hide…
because we're all ooey-gooey and cheesy,
   deep down inside.

A special thank you to

Pedone's Pizza in Redondo Beach,

for bringing me friendships and love

that I will cherish forever.